E
Lu

The Gift of Ramadan

Rabiah York Lumbard

illustrated by

Laura K. Horton

Albert Whitman & Company
Chicago, Illinois

A rainbow of color winked at Sophia as she handed the Ramadan lights to her momma. These were her favorite decorations, because they made her feel as though a special guest was coming.

Grandma raised an eyebrow. "Pretty," she said. "Pretty and sparkly. Just like the heart of a person who fasts."

Sophia stopped twirling. "Really?" she asked. Sophia loved sparkles. Glitter. Stars. Her new ring. It was a gift from Grandma for her birthday last month.

Grandma stopped rocking. "Really."

Sophia knew that fasting was to not eat or drink
from sunup to sundown. Sophia loved food. But she also
loved sparkles.

She turned to her momma. "When does Ramadan begin?"

Momma opened the curtain.

Adam, Sophia's little brother, pointed to the sky.

"Moooooon," he said.

"That's right," Momma answered. "See how thin it is?"

Sophia nodded.

"That's the crescent moon, the beginning of a new month. Tomorrow is the first day of fasting."

"Count me in!" Sophia grinned.

Momma woke Sophia when it was so early not even the sun was awake! "Time for *sahoor*!" she sang.

Sophia sat down to a breakfast of eggs, fruit, and Dad's pancakes.
But Sophia could barely keep her eyes open.

"You have to eat!" Grandma told her. "It will chase away the hungries."

Sophia reached for a pancake. But a few minutes later...

"Time's up!" Dad said.

They got up from the table and unrolled the prayer rugs, one by one.

Sophia tried her best to stay awake, but the moment her head
touched the ground, sleep came over her.

Momma reached forward to nudge her, but Grandma waved
her finger to say, *Let her sleep!*

When Sophia woke for the second time, it was almost noon.
Her tummy was empty, and her throat was dry. But even drinking
water was against the rules.

So, Sophia decided to stay busy.

She read for a while.

She organized the clothes in her closet—from least to most sparkly.

And then she drew. But her tummy began to gurgle louder and louder.
"Shh!" Sophia said, "I'm drawing."
She glanced down at her paper.
"Yikes," she said. "I've got to get out of here!"

Sophia found Adam in front of the TV. In his hand was a humongous cookie. He waved it in front of her face and sang, "Me cookie eat! Yummy. Yum. Yum."

Sophia's tummy roared. The cookie looked delicious. "Please stop," she said, but Adam kept singing. Sophia clenched her hands. She bit her lip. She wanted to yell. Instead she ran out of the room. Her brother chased her.

Adam was fast, but Sophia was faster.
Sophia was so fast she ran out of breath!
She needed to hide. Adam was still looking for her.

Sophia turned on the light. "Oh no!" she thought. "I've really got to get out of here." But she couldn't. Adam was stomping by. Still singing that song.

"Me cookie eat! Yummy. Yum. Yum."

She plugged her ears. She closed her eyes. Sophia took a deep breath—and the scent of chocolate filled her nose!

"What is this?" asked Grandma.

Sophia's eyes drifted to the floor. "I got too hungry."

"There, there, my love. No one expects you to fast for an entire day." Grandma wrapped Sophia in a big hug. "There's always tomorrow and the day after and the next. You have a full month to keep trying."

Sophia twisted her ring. She wiped away her tears. "But I wanted to feel sparkly now," she said.

"You are sparkly!" Grandma said. "I can see your sparkles growing."

Sophia shrugged. She didn't feel sparkly.

"And did you know," continued Grandma, "there are other ways to celebrate Ramadan?"

Sophia thought about that. She knew Momma read the Quran.
Maybe it gave her head sparkles. But Sophia couldn't read it.
Not on her own.

And her dad was always sharing things with family, friends, and strangers. He said that Ramadan was a time for charity, a special kind of sharing for those who need extra help. But Sophia didn't have any money.

Sophia was about to give up when she glanced down at Grandma's hands. They were covered in flour. "What are you making?" she asked. "Yummy food for our first *iftar*," Grandma replied.

"That's it!" Sophia thought. If she couldn't fast, then at least she could help prepare dinner for those who did.

"And I'm going to help!"

Sophia put on her apron and got to work. She tossed the salad.
Then she helped Grandma make five super-sparkly pizzas—one for
each member of the family. Sophia thought they were sparkly because
they had extra cheese on them. Grandma thought it was the fresh
parsley that made them shine.

When the oven buzzed, Sophia jumped up from her chair. The pizzas were finally done. But when Grandma opened the oven, smoke billowed out.

"Oh no!" Sophia frowned.

The top three pizzas were perfect. But the bottom two were burnt to a crisp.

Grandma plopped down. She looked exhausted. Iftar was just around the corner.

"Don't worry, Grandma," said Sophia. "I've got this!"

"Really?" asked Grandma.

"Really," said Sophia.

Sophia set the table. She gave each person one big bowl of soup and one salad. She placed a pitcher of water and a bowl of dates on the table. Then she asked Grandma to cut up the three perfect pizzas. Tiny slices were better than none.

Sophia's family gathered around the table. They raised their hands and offered thanks. Then they each drank water and ate a date.

When there was only one slice of pizza left, Grandma insisted that Sophia take it. "You've earned it!"

"No thanks." Sophia smiled. She didn't want any more.
She didn't need any more. Her heart was wonderfully full.

Author's Note

Ramadan is the ninth month of the Islamic calendar and the fourth pillar of Islam. The month is holy to Muslims because they believe it was during this time the first verses of the Quran, the Islamic holy book, were spoken to the Prophet Muhammad by the angel Gabriel. Many people, like Sophia's mom, try to finish reading the Quran by the end of the month. Ramadan is also called the month of mercy and the month of forgiveness, which is why Sophia's dad might give to charity.

Ramadan commences with the sighting of the crescent moon. During this sacred month, Muslims fast from sunup to sundown—refraining from taking food and drink. Muslims prepare for the fast each day by waking up before the sun and eating a wholesome breakfast called *sahoor*. They end the fast each day at dusk with a family or community dinner called *iftar*. Iftar is often followed by prayers called *tarawih*, which extend long into the night.

While the age at which a Muslim begins to fast may vary from household to household, full observance is generally expected around puberty. However, from the ages of seven and up, many children will try to fast for a few hours. Each year they fast a little bit longer. Those who are not required to fast *at all* are the very young, the ill, the elderly, pregnant or nursing women, and those who are traveling.

The famous teacher Ahmad al-Ghazali once said that there are three kinds of fasts. The first concerns the body. This fast is the most basic fast and is explained above. The second includes the first then adds to it the fast of one's actions and speech. People watch closely what they do and what they say, like when Sophia refrained from yelling at her brother. The third kind of fast is the fast of the heart—to be utterly selfless. The month is about emptying oneself of all that is selfish, then filling oneself with all that is good, true, and beautiful. Just like Sophia did.

For Kevin O'Connor, friend and agent, who found me
in a slush pile and never looked back.—RYL

To Mom—my own spiritual guide—LKH

Library of Congress Cataloging-in-Publication data is on file with the publisher.

Text copyright © 2019 by Rabiah York Lumbard
Illustrations copyright © 2019 by Albert Whitman & Company
Illustrations by Laura K. Horton
First published in the United States of America in 2019 by Albert Whitman & Company
ISBN 978-0-8075-2906-5

Printed in China
10 9 8 7 6 5 4 3 2 1 HH 22 21 20 19 18

Design by Aphee Messer

For more information about Albert Whitman & Company,
visit our website at www.albertwhitman.com.

100 Years of Albert Whitman & Company
Celebrate with us in 2019!